PLENTY OF LOVE TO GO AROUND

Emma Chichester Clark

 NANCY PAULSEN BOOKS

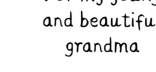

For my young
and beautiful
grandma

NANCY PAULSEN BOOKS
an imprint of Penguin Random House LLC
375 Hudson Street
New York, NY 10014

Copyright © 2016 by Emma Chichester Clark.
First American edition published in 2016 by Nancy Paulsen Books.
Also published in Great Britain in 2016 by Random House Children's Publishers UK.
Penguin supports copyright. Copyright fuels creativity, encourages diverse voices, promotes free speech, and creates a vibrant culture.
Thank you for buying an authorized edition of this book and for complying with copyright laws by not reproducing, scanning, or distributing
any part of it in any form without permission. You are supporting writers and allowing Penguin to continue to publish books for every reader.

Nancy Paulsen Books is a registered trademark of Penguin Random House LLC.

Library of Congress Cataloging-in-Publication Data is available upon request.

Manufactured in China.
ISBN 978-0-399-54666-2
Special Markets ISBN 978-1-524-73852-5
1 3 5 7 9 10 8 6 4 2

The art was done in watercolor and colored pencil.

This Imagination Library edition is published by Penguin Young Readers, a division
of Penguin Random House, exclusively for Dolly Parton's Imagination Library,
a not-for-profit program designed to inspire a love of reading and learning, sponsored
in part by The Dollywood Foundation. Penguin's trade editions of this work are
available wherever books are sold.

I AM PLUM.

The one and only special Plum.

Emma and Rupert are my family, and I just love them.

When they say I am their Special One, I feel loved all over.

Sam and Gracie live next door. They are my best friends, and I am their **best** one and only.

But one day, Gracie said, "We've got a surprise for you, Plum!"

"This is Binky!"
said Sam.

He was holding
a cat.

Cats are **not** my favorite thing.

"He loves you, Plum! Don't you **LOVE** him?"
asked Gracie.
"We love him!" said Sam.

I was so happy to go to the park.
The park is just for dogs.

"I say!" said my friend Esther.
"Is that cat with you?"

I couldn't believe it!

"Who's your new friend?" asked Rocket.
"He's not my friend!" I said.

"Well, he's following you!" said Bean.

"Scat, cat!" I said.

When I got home,
guess who was there?
"It's nice to have a cat
around," said Emma.

No! It isn't! It isn't!

The cat followed me everywhere,

sniffed where I sniffed,

rolled where I rolled,

peed when I peed,

stretched when
I stretched.

I couldn't
get away!

I went to the shed to hide.

But the cat followed me there too . . .

When the door slammed shut, we were stuck!

"Meow!" he said, and off he went.

"CATS!" I said.

Now no one will ever find me.

But I was wrong
about that, because
Binky came back with
Sam and Gracie.

They told Emma
and Rupert.
"Clever Binky!"
said Rupert.

"He's SO clever!"
said Sam.

He's just a **CAT!** Nothing
special about that!

"Oh, look at Binky!"
said Gracie as he
ran up a tree.

"He can do **anything!**"
said Sam.

It's true. It's really
true, I thought.

Now Binky was the Special One.

I thought he was a **show-off**, clever-clogs cat.

"He's ruining everything!"
I told Esther.

"Have you tried
being friends?"
asked Jakey.

"I can't be friends with a cat!" I told Bean.

"What if they love him more than **me**?" I asked Rocket.

"Oh, there's **plenty** of love to go around," he said.

But I wasn't sure.

Sam and Gracie were watching TV.

The cat was outside.

He came back when he saw me.

So I pushed the door shut and leaned against the cat flap.

"Stop following me!" I told him.

"Stay out till I say so."

Just then, Emma and Rupert came.

They found little Binky . . .

and then they saw me in front of the cat flap.

I looked at Emma and she looked at me. She knew what I'd done.

"Now, Plummie," Emma said. "You will always be my Special One . . . but you're going to **have** to be nice to the cat!

There's room in our hearts for him and for **YOU!**"

"You've got a big heart, haven't you, Plummie?" said Emma.

And suddenly I could feel it growing.
It grew **BIGGER** and **BIGGER**.

I have a big heart! I do. I do!
And now I know—
there's enough love for two . . .

In fact, there's PLENTY of love
to go around and around! Yes,
there's plenty of love to go around.

For Jon,
who wears the finest **socks**
N. S.

For the **sockalicious** Arthur, Florence and Cecily,
with my love
E. L.

The refrain in this book was inspired by the wonderfully named
Choccywoccydoodah, a chocolaterie in Brighton

A PICTURE CORGI BOOK
SOCKS
978 0 552 57221 7

First published in Great Britain
by David Fickling Books in
2012. This Picture Corgi
edition published 2016.

4 6 8 10 11 9 7 5 3

Text copyright © Nick Sharratt
and Elizabeth Lindsay, 2012
Illustrations copyright ©
Nick Sharratt, 2012

The right of Elizabeth Lindsay
and Nick Sharratt to be
identified as the author and
illustrator of this work has
been asserted in
accordance with the Copyright,
Designs and Patents Act 1988.

All rights reserved. No
part of this publication
may be reproduced, stored
in a retrieval system,
or transmitted in any
form or by any means,
electronic, mechanical,
photocopying, recording or
otherwise, without the prior
permission of the publishers.

Picture Corgi Books are published
by Random House Children's Publishers,
61–63 Uxbridge Road, London W5 5SA

www.randomhousechildrens.co.uk
www.randomhouse.co.uk

Addresses for companies within The Random
House Group Limited can be found at:
www.randomhouse.co.uk/offices.htm
THERANDOMHOUSEGROUPLimitedReg.No.954009

A CIP catalogue record for this book is
available from the British Library.

Printed in China

MIX
Paper from
responsible sources
FSC
www.fsc.org   FSC® C018179

Socks

Written by
Nick Sharratt & Elizabeth Lindsay

Illustrated by
Nick Sharratt

Picture Corgi

SOCKYWOCKYDOODAH!

A-tick-a-tick-a-tock

What's the time in **Sockland?**

It's always **SOCKS O'CLOCK!**

SOCKYWOCKYDOODAH!

The **sockerel** struts his stuff

And **sock-a-bloomin'-doodles**

Till the hens cry, **"THAT'S ENOUGH!"**

Put a sock in it!

Nice horsies

SOCKYWOCKYDOODAH!
The happy cows go **MOO**

Sockish ponies, aren't they sweet?

And teeny tiny too.

SOCKYWOCKYDOODAH!

So what do we have here?

A greedy-guts called **Goldisocks**

And three cross bears, **OH DEAR!**

SOCKYWOCKY-CHOOCHOO-TRAIN!

For **Socktown** take a seat
There everybody's wearing **socks**
And not just on their **FEET!**

SOCKYWOCKYDOODAH!
Popsock-a-lula-bop!
That **socksophone** just makes you feel
Like **JIVING** till you drop!

Sock 'n' Roll!

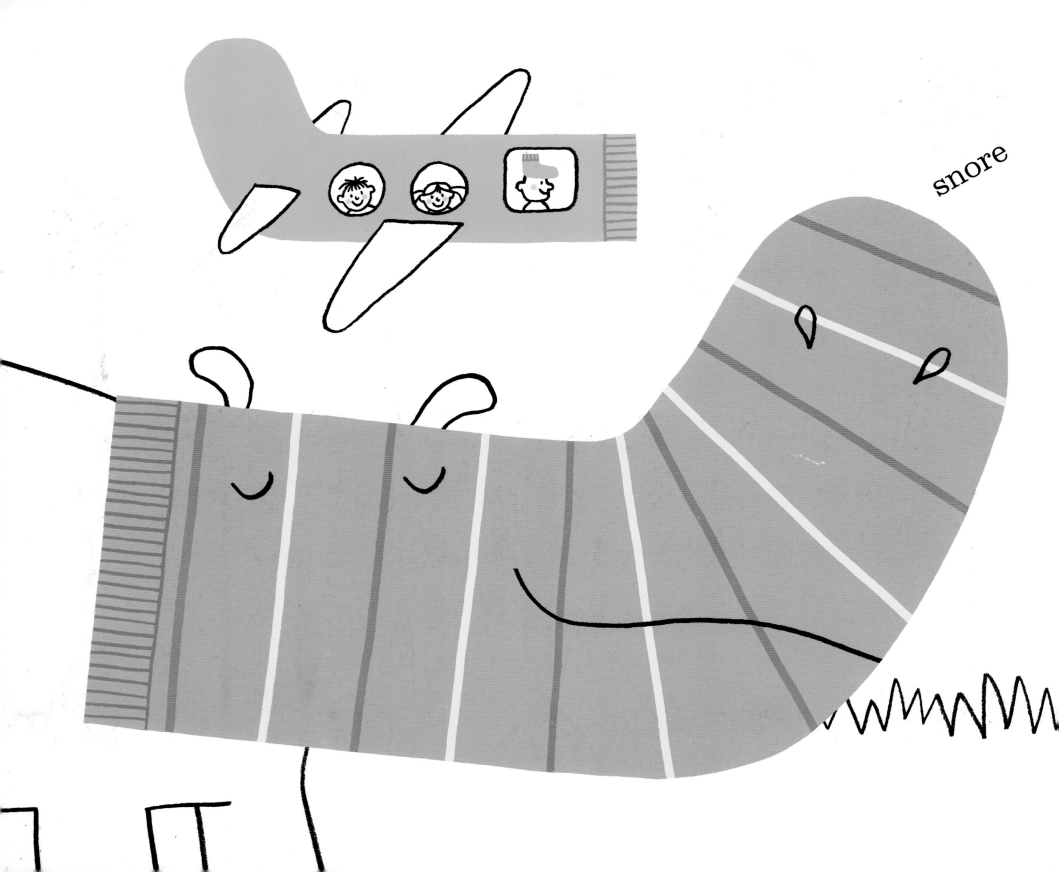

snore

SOCKYWOCK-ADVENTURE!

From our **sock plane** we can spy

A dozing **hipposockamus**

As **sockatoos** fly by.

SOCKYWOCKY-SNAP-SNAP!

Beware the **sockodile**

Especially when she flashes you

Her **socking** GREAT BIG SMILE!

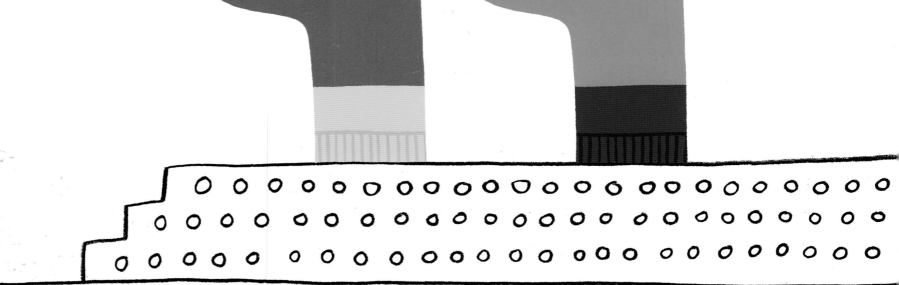

SOCKYWOCKY-ALL-ABOARD!

Let's cruise the **socky seas**

What lies beneath the salty waves?

We'd like an **ANSWER** please!

mmm, tasty!

SOCKYWOCKYDOODAH!
By our little **sockmarine**
There's a **socktopus**, a **mersock**
And a **sockshark** looking **MEAN!**

tra-la-la!

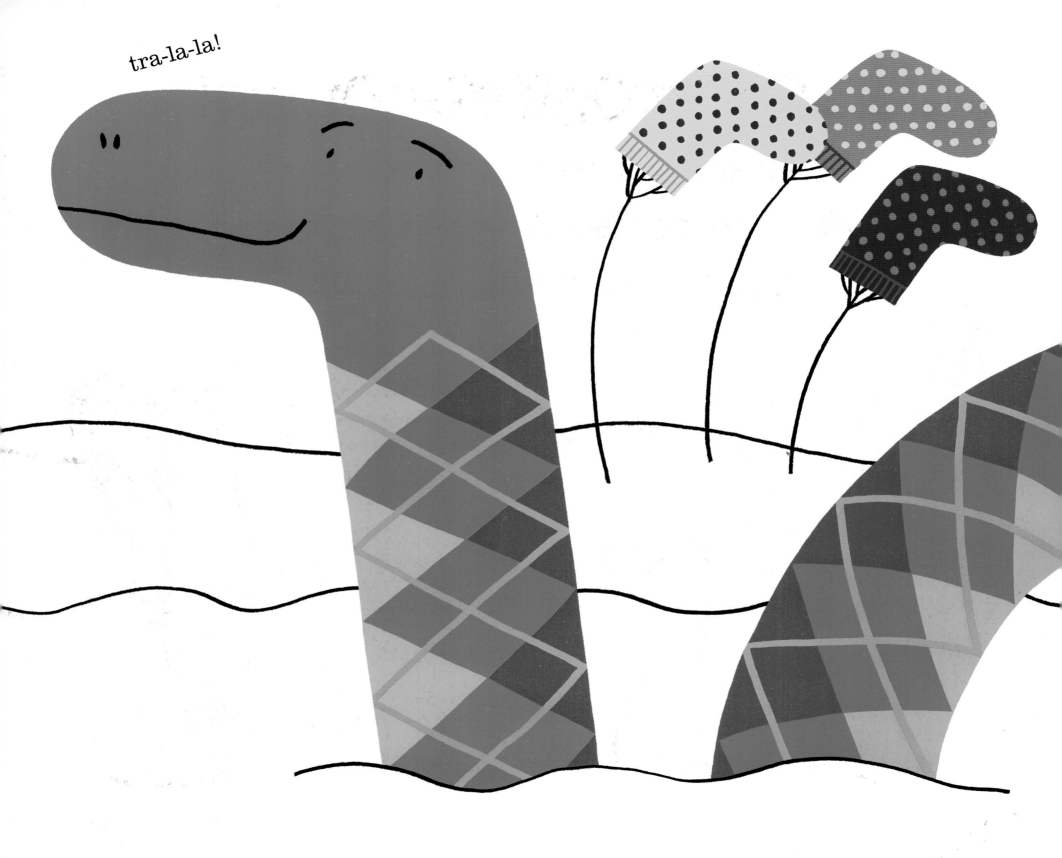

SOCKYWOCKYDOODAH!

As **sock trees** gently sway

Wave to the **Sock Ness Monster**

On her summer holiday!

SOCKYWOCKY-SLEEPY-YAWN!

It's **bedsocks** time, OK?

We've had the most

SOCKTASTIC,

sockalicious,

SOCK-ELASTIC,

socks-amazing,

SOCKS-A-CRAZY,

sock-a-zooming,

SOCK-A-WAVY,

Sock-it-to-me-round-the-clocky

SOCKYWOCKYDOODAH-DAY!

(phew!)

More books illustrated
by Nick Sharratt:

JUST
IMAGINE

Nick Sharratt   Pippa Goodhart
Let your imagination run wild – what will you choose to be!

YOU
CHOOSE

Nick Sharratt   Pippa Goodhart

Giles
Andreae   Nick
Sharratt

Pants

Giles
Andreae   Nick
Sharratt

more
Pants

A fin-tastic sequel to Shark in the Park!

Shark
in the
Dark!

GLOWS
in the
DARK!

Nick Sharratt

Shark
in the
Dark!

Nick Sharratt